# Zoey
## and the Magical Hummingbirds

## Eboniè P Fields

AuthorHouse™
1663 Liberty Drive
Bloomington, IN 47403
www.authorhouse.com
Phone: 833-262-8899

Because of the dynamic nature of the Internet, any web addresses or links contained in this book may have changed since publication and may no longer be valid. The views expressed in this work are solely those of the author and do not necessarily reflect the views of the publisher, and the publisher hereby disclaims any responsibility for them.

Any people depicted in stock imagery provided by Getty Images are models, and such images are being used for illustrative purposes only.
Certain stock imagery © Getty Images.

This book is printed on acid-free paper.

ISBN: 978-1-6655-1041-7 (sc)
ISBN: 978-1-6655-1040-0 (e)

Print information available on the last page.

Library of Congress Control Number: 2020924427

Published by AuthorHouse 12/08/2020

authorHOUSE

Once upon a time in the country hills of Jamaica, there lived a beautiful young girl named Zoey with her two loving parents. They lived in a modest, one-story, pastel-pink house. Bright white paint outlined the windows and doors of their home. In the garden grew luscious green bushes with vibrant red and yellow flowers. In the middle of the front yard stood a mango tree on which was hung a homemade wooden swing.

Zoey was swinging, starring down at the hot-pink sandals that matched her hot-pink pants. Her yellow and pink polka-dotted blouse was accessorized with a bright yellow bow. She slowly swung back and forth with no excitement or delight. She looked at pink balloons and a yard sign that said, "Baby Girl." Zoey was saddened by the fact that her parents were welcoming a new baby girl into the family. For years, she was the only child in the family, swimming, playing, shopping, and eating with her parents. She could feel their attention and love drifting away from her and to the new baby.

She said to herself, "They don't want me here anymore. My new baby sister is all they need. I am going to just leave and go to a place where I am loved." Zoey quickly ran through the house unnoticed as her parents gazed at her newborn baby sister with joy. Zoey entered her room, which was full of dolls and family pictures of her and her parents at the zoo, on the beach, and at home. She grabbed her pink backpack and filled it with clothes, and most important, with her lucky green blanket, twenty dollars, and another pair of pink sandals. Once she was packed, Zoey sneaked out the back door of the house and quickly began to walk up the road full of sandy rocks and pebbles.

As Zoey walked, she gazed up into the clear blue skies, clutching her backpack close. As she looked at the sky, she saw two small hummingbirds flying above her. They were only about four and a half inches tall. The body of the bird on the right was covered with beautiful, florescent, bright-green feathers. The hummingbird had a long, bright-red bill with a black tip that matched the crown of its head. Two long feathers on its tail hung down about ten inches. The other bird did not have a tail hanging down. It was slightly smaller and had light green and black feathers, a pearl-white chest, and a long black bill.

"Hello, my name is Alizabeth, but you can call me Izzy," said the black-billed hummingbird in a sweet soft voice. "And this is my friend, Louie."

"Hello," said Louie in a chipper and friendly voice.

"Hello. My name is Zoey. Nice to meet you both," she said.

"Where are you going, sweetheart?" asked Izzy.

"I'm running away from home so that I can live in a house where I am special and not ignored."

"That is your reason for leaving?" asked Louie.

"I'm ready for more excitement, fun, and adventure anyway," Zoey added.

"So you're going to run away and leave this beautiful home to search for excitement, fun, and adventure," said Louie. "I don't know if that is a good idea, kid. What about your family and home?"

"I will find somewhere better, where I'm not forgotten," replied Zoey. "I'm bored at home now that my parents are giving all their attention to the new baby. I am going to see new places and new things. Wherever I go next, I will be the special one, not a new baby."

"Okay, sweetheart. So new places and new things are what you are looking for. We can help you with that," said Izzy. "Right, Louie?"

"Yes, we can show you some new places and new things," Louie said.

"Wow, you two can?" Zoey asked, with a hopeful smile on her face.

"Yes. We just need you to close your eyes and repeat after us," said Izzy.

Zoey stood in the middle of a dusty road, smiled up at the two hummingbirds, and closed her eyes. "Okay, let's go," she said.

Izzy and Louie then began to quickly fly around Zoey, singing,

Up, up, and away we fly,

above the trees into the sky.

Over the waterfalls, lakes, and mountains,

we fly across the rivers and gardens.

To and fro we spread our wings,

in hopes to see new places and things.

"Open your eyes," said Izzy.

Zoey was standing under a beautiful canopy of trees. She looked around and quickly realized that she was in the middle of a rain forest. There were all shades of green and all types of colorful flowers, ranging from bright orange to fluorescent pink to purple, blue, and yellow. As Zoey looked on in amazement, a beautiful black-and-yellow butterfly with a speckled tail of blue spots flew by. Zoey began to chase the butterfly in hopes of getting it to land on her finger. But as she ran faster and faster, she lost sight of the objects in front of her. Then suddenly, *boooom!* She bumped into another little girl running through the rain forest.

"I'm so sorry. I didn't see you," Zoey said. "I was chasing a butterfly."

"No problem," responded the other girl. "My name is Sandy."

"Hello, Sandy. My name is Zoey."

"So do you love butterflies?" asked Sandy.

"Yes, I do," answered Zoey. "My mom and I love to get the butterflies to land on our fingers."

"Follow me," said Sandy. "But first … Tag, you're it!" Joyfully, Sandy tapped Zoey on the shoulder and began running into the tropical bushes of the rain forest. Sandy yelled, "You can't catch me," giggling as she began running out of sight.

Zoey chased after her, curious to see where she would run to next. Together, they ran quickly through the forest, laughing and passing through beautiful tropical flowers such as Jamaican orchids and hibiscus. When Zoey finally caught up to Sandy, she found her hunched over a bushy tropical plant, staring through a small opening of the bush. Sandy whispered, "Come over here. I want to show you something." She pushed a band of bushes to the left and then carefully walked through them. Zoey followed, and as she raised her head out of the bushes, she saw a blue-green lagoon filled by a nearby flowing waterfall. The lagoon stood in the middle of a natural garden of more green tropical plants, ferns, and a colorful rainbow of tropical flowers that bloomed all around her. Zoey and Sandy picked out bouquets of flowers, smelling each bud they picked. As Zoey looked around, she saw a variety of butterflies fluttering their wings above her. The butterflies ranged from orange and black, yellow and black, blue and yellow, and red and black.

"How did you know about this place?" Zoey asked.

"I come here all the time," answered Sandy. "Ever since my dad died from a sickness the doctors couldn't cure, it has just been my mom and me. My mom always has to go to work, and I come out here so I don't feel so lonely. I don't feel so alone when I'm around the butterflies and singing with the birds." Sandy smiled.

"Oh. Well, I'm glad you found this place, Sandy. It is beautiful. It's definitely a great place to catch butterflies," said Zoey with a huge smile.

As Zoey walked along the lagoon, she shouted, "I love this place!" Then suddenly, they both heard an animal whimpering nearby.

"Did you hear that?" asked Zoey.

"Yes," answered Sandy. "It's over to our right, closer to the lagoon. Look!" shouted Sandy. There in the wet grasslands near the lagoon whimpered a cute brown-and-black puppy that looked to weigh no more than five pounds.

"It's a little puppy. How did it get here?" Zoey wondered. "We need to give it a home."

"I will give this cute little puppy a home and feed him well," said Sandy, holding him close to her. "I will take good care of him, play with him, and treat him like family. I just wish I had something to wrap him in."

"Here," said Zoey. She pulled her lucky green blanket out of her backpack. "Wrap this around him, and carry him safely home."

"I'm going to go ahead and get home and feed him some food. I enjoyed playing with you and exploring the rain forest. Get home to your family safely," said Sandy.

"Bye-bye, Sandy!" yelled Zoey.

"Looks like someone made a new friend," said Izzy, swooping down above Zoey.

"Yes, it was nice playing with a new friend."

"Well, are you ready to see some more new places and new things?" asked Louie.

"Yes," exclaimed Zoey, closing her eyes.

Izzy and Louie then began to quickly fly around Zoey, again singing,

Up, up, and away we fly,

above the trees into the sky.

Over the waterfalls, lakes, and mountains,

we fly across the rivers and gardens.

To and fro we spread our wings,

in hopes to see new places and things.

"Open your eyes," said Izzy.

Zoey opened her eyes. In front of her was a huge cave. In the outside entrance of the cave stood a young boy yelling "Tommy! Tommy! Where are you?"

Zoey slowly walked up to the young boy and asked, "Did you lose someone?"

"Yes, my little brother," answered the boy. "I have to find him. He is my world, my buddy, and my best friend. Plus, my parents are going to be terribly upset with me if I've lost him. I have to find him."

"Okay. I'm Zoey, and I will help you find him," she said looking into the cave.

"Thank you, Zoey. I'm Shawn."

"It's nice to meet you, Shawn. Let's go find your little brother."

Slowly, Shawn and Zoey walked into the dark cave. A few rays of sunlight shone through large holes in the cave. With shaking legs and fearful faces, they put one foot in front of the other and slowly walked deeper into the cave.

"Where do you think he could be?" asked Zoey. "The cave is bigger inside than I thought it would be."

"I don't know, "answered Shawn. "Let's just keep on yelling his name."

"Tommmy! Tommmy!" they both yelled in desperation.

"Did you hear that?" Zoey asked.

"What? I don't hear anything."

"A tapping sound," Zoey explained.

Slowly, they turned to their right, and a group of bats flew around them, passing through a tunnel in the cave. Zoey screamed for dear life, "Ahhhhhh! Ahhhhhh!"

"It was just a camp of bats," Shawn said, laughing at Zoey. "That's what a group of bats is called."

"What are you kids doing in dis cave? Here there are only ghosts and bats dat misbehave," asked a short, frail old man with a heavy Jamaican accent. He walked with a carved dark-brown wooden cane. Hummingbirds and vines twisted from the top to the bottom of his cane. His long, dark-brown and gray locks fell past his shoulders and matched his long, dark-brown and gray beard. The man walked with a limp and wore old, dirty, cut-off jeans and an old, dark-blue T-shirt that appeared to be too big for him.

"We are just here looking for my little brother. Who are you?" Shawn asked.

"Search your soul dat is within thee, your lost one is not far from you to see," rhymed the old man.

Shawn and Zoey looked at each other in confusion and then back at the old man with concern. "Really? Who are you, and why do you like to rhyme?" asked Zoey.

"Don't worry who I am or my story. Be concerned with the cave that holds all the mystery and history," the old man replied.

"Obviously, this man has been in here too long," said Shawn.

"He does speak some truth. I remember my granny telling me a story about the caves here in Jamaica," said Zoey. "She once told me that the caves used to be a hiding place for the Arawak Indians, who used to hide from Christopher Columbus and his men in the late 1400s. Columbus landed here in May of 1494, hoping to find riches for Spain. Granny also told me that the Arawak Indians hid their gems, jewelry, and crystals in the caves to keep them from pirates that anchored at Port Royal. Some people say that their spirits still live in the cave to protect their hidden treasures."

"Many ships have set for sea in hopes to find riches that might be, but a pirate's glossy gems, gold, and treasures will never be or even measure to the love of family that endures forever," sang the old man.

"Okay, let's find my brother and get out of here," Shawn said as he looked at the old man in bewilderment.

"Mister, have you seen a little boy?" asked Zoey.

"Search your soul dat is within thee. Your lost one is not far from you to see," the old man riddled again.

"I think I know where he is," said Shawn. "He always talks about seeing the lake in the cave. Let's listen for running water, splashes, or drops of water."

"To the left," answered Zoey. "I hear splashing."

"It must be my brother. Thank you, mister, but we've got it from here," said Shawn.

"I'm just an old man with wisdom and knowledge, to give truth to those who will acknowledge," said the old man. He smiled at Shawn and Zoey, showing the four teeth in his mouth, and slowly walked backward into a dark shadow.

"That was weird," said Shawn.

"Yes, it was. Let's just hurry up and find your brother," said Zoey.

Shawn and Zoey walked slowly through a dark tunnel of the cave. And at the other end of the tunnel swam Shawn's little brother, Tommy.

"Tommy!" called Shawn. Tommy waved back with a huge smile on his face. "What are you doing? Let's get out of here," yelled Shawn. Shawn and Zoey walked over to Tommy and pulled him out of the lake, dripping wet. "Let's go!" said Shawn.

"Hi, Tommy. I am Zoey," she cheerfully introduced herself. "Your brother was really worried about you. I'm glad you are safe."

"Nice to meet you," replied Tommy.

They all walked out of the cave and back into the bright sunny day and beautiful tropical weather.

"I'm glad we're out of that cave," Shawn said with relief.

"I'm hungry," cried Tommy.

"I'm a little hungry myself," said Shawn. "I just don't have any money on me."

"I do," yelled Zoey, pulling her twenty dollars out of her backpack. "Let's go and get something to eat."

They walked a couple of miles to a local restaurant. During the walk, Shawn talked about all the fun games and sports that he and Tommy liked to play together. Zoey just listened quietly. When they arrived at the restaurant, each ordered a kid's plate of curry chicken and rice. As they ate, Zoey saw the joy and laughter shared between Tommy and Shawn. She began to feel left out and out of place. Zoey slowly got up from her chair. "Well, I have to go," she said as she pushed her chair into the table.

"What?" asked Shawn. "You just got here. You didn't even finish your food."

"It's fine. I'm full anyway," replied Zoey. "I have somewhere I must be. It was nice meeting you both."

"Nice meeting you too," said Shawn, quickly getting out of his chair to give Zoey a big, long hug. "Thank you for everything today, Zoey. God bless you."

"Anytime, Shawn. Well you two have fun for the rest of your day," she said with a smile.

Zoey raced out of the restaurant. As soon as she got outside, Izzy and Louie flew down to greet her.

"So how was your time in the cave?" asked Louie.

"So did you find adventure?" asked Izzy.

"Yes, you can say that. It was a cool experience," replied Zoey.

"Well are you ready to see more new places and new things?" asked Louie.

"Yes," said Zoey, closing her eyes.

Izzy and Louie quickly began to fly around Zoey, singing,

Up, up, and away we fly,

above the trees into the sky.

Over the waterfalls, lakes, and mountains,

we fly across the rivers and gardens.

To and fro we spread our wings,

in hopes to see new places and things.

"Open your eyes," said Izzy.

When Zoey opened her eyes, in front of her was a clear blue-green ocean filled with people from all around the world. They were swimming, jumping, and playing.

As she walked to the ocean to touch the water, a ball rolled in front of her. As she stopped to pick it up, a young boy ran over to her, a young girl next to him.

"Sorry about that," said the boy, wearing blue-and-white swim shorts and a blue T-shirt. "My family and I were just kicking the ball around. Do you want to play?"

Zoey nodded.

"I'm Zenie, and this is little my sister, Anna." Zenie walked Zoey over to the rest of the family and introduced her to his parents, Mr. and Mrs. Goldie, and his brother, Peter. After she met everyone, she began playing with Zenie's family, kicking the ball back and forth. She laughed and enjoyed the togetherness that Zenie's family had.

"We're finished playing on the beach. We're going to climb the waterfalls behind you as a family," said Zenie. "Do you want to come?"

"I would love to," answered Zoey. "That sounds like fun."

"Great! My family and I love to climb the waterfalls together. As we climb the falls, we hold hands to make sure that nobody falls," Zenie explained. Zoey looked closer at the gushing waterfall, and saw several families holding hands, smiling, and laughing as they climbed about a 180-foot waterfall.

"I need my sandals," cried Anna. "I cannot climb the rocks barefoot. It will hurt my feet."

"Don't worry," yelled Zoey. "I have an extra pair of sandals you can have. They should fit you." She pulled out her pink pair of sandals and handed them to Anna.

"Thank you so much," Anna said with a smile of relief over her face.

Zoey smiled at Anna and looked back at the waterfall full of joyful families holding hands. "You're welcome," she said. "I have to go."

"What about the waterfall?" asked Zenie.

"Maybe some other time," yelled Zoey as she walked backward off the beach. "I had a lot of fun playing with you and your family. But now it's time for me to return to mine."

As Zoey walked away, Izzy and Louie came flying down to her. "So how was your day?" Izzy asked.

"It was fun and adventurous. But now I miss my family and want to go home," said Zoey.

"It sounds like someone has found true wisdom today," said Louie.

"Yes," agreed Izzy. "Family is a precious gift that is more important than jewels, gems, and riches. The Lord blessed you with a family who loves you and wants the best for you."

"I see that now," said Zoey. "I guess I was jealous of my new baby sister, and I didn't think about the fact that she will be fun to play with and take care of."

"Your parents have had a new baby girl, which is a blessing to you and your family. Treasure the gifts that God has given you, and you will find peace and love in your heart," promised Izzy.

"Let's get you home, kid," said Louie.

Izzy and Louie quickly flew around Zoey, singing,

Up, up, and away we fly,

above the trees into the sky.

Over the waterfalls, lakes, and mountains,

we fly across the rivers and gardens.

To and fro we spread our wings,

in hopes to see new places and things.

"Open your eyes," said Izzy.

Zoey stood in front of a white picket fence that surrounded her home. She quickly opened the fence, ran through the porch to the door, and swung the door open. "Mom, Dad, I'm home," she yelled with joy.

Her mother ran over to her and squeezed her tight. "We were so worried about you, Zoey. Don't do that to us again."

"I won't. I am so sorry, Mom and Dad. I know that home is where love and happiness are for me. I love you. I love my family."

"We love you too. Always remember, Zoey, that you are loved," said Zoey's mom.

Zoey walked over to her father, who sat on a long green couch, holding her baby sister. Zoey hugged her dad and leaned over to kiss her baby sister. As she did, Zoey whispered, "I'm going be the best big sister ever and show you so much love."

"What did you decide to name the baby?" Zoey asked.

"We named her Adeline, after your great-grandmother, whom you love to call Granny," answered Zoey's mom. "She was a wonderful and wise woman."

"It's a beautiful name," Zoey said. "It's perfect for her."

The family spent a quiet evening, just sitting on the couch and looking at baby Adeline. Each took turns talking and playing with her as Louie and Izzy gazed through the window.

"Look at those two beautiful hummingbirds at the window," said Zoey's mom. They are called streamer tail hummingbirds, and they are known to be the most beautiful birds in Jamaica. Your granny used to tell me an old Jamaican folklore that was told by the Arawak Indians centuries ago. The Arawak Indians used to believe these hummingbirds had magical powers and referred to them as God's birds."

Zoey looked at Izzy and Louie through the living room window and smiled. With a huge smile on her face she said, "I can believe that. They truly are God's birds."

# About the Author

Eboniè P. Fields is a poet, writer, and children's book author. Fields enjoys using her writing talents to create exciting and vivid stories for children of all ages to read. She has the creative talent to descriptively allow your imagination to put you inside the story, taking you on an incredible journey with her charismatic characters.

Fields has a bachelor of arts degree in journalism from Baylor University and a master's in business administration with a concentration in marketing from Texas Women's University. In 2008, she was awarded the Rising Star in Women in Radio & Television and selected as a nominee for Houston Business Journal's 40 under 40 Award in 2014.

Fields resides in Phoenix, Arizona, with her husband and two adorable kids. Her volunteer work in the community has driven her passion to write stories and poems that bring joy and adventure to children around the world.

CPSIA information can be obtained
at www.ICGtesting.com
Printed in the USA
LVHW071121190121
676816LV00025B/378